RAY
and the
Best Family Reunion Ever

Mildred Pitts Walter

📕 HarperCollins*Publishers*

Amistad

Library of Congress Cataloging-in-Publication Data
Walter, Mildred Pitts.
Ray and the best family reunion ever / Mildred Pitts Walter.
p.   cm.
Summary: When his family attends a reunion in Louisiana, eleven-
year-old Ray learns about his Creole roots and about the circum-
stances that have kept him from ever meeting his father's father.
ISBN 0-06-623624-X — ISBN 0-06-623625-8 (lib. bdg.)
[1. Family reunions—Fiction. 2. Fathers and sons—Fiction.
3. Grandfathers—Fiction. 4. Creoles—Fiction.] I. Title.
PZ7.W17125 Ray 2002   2001024600
[Fic]—dc21   CIP
                                                                AC

Typography by Larissa Lawrynenko
1 2 3 4 5 6 7 8 9 10
❖
First Edition

j Fic

Contents

1

A Strange Phone Call

LATE IN THE EVENING, the telephone rang. Ray rushed to answer it, but his papa had already picked up. Ray heard his angry voice and stopped. "I've told you don't call here. So don't, ever again." He slammed down the receiver. He hit his fist in his hand, shook his head, and walked past Ray without seeing him.

Who could that have been? Ray wondered, watching his father go down the hall, back to bed. Papa was not the kind to show that much anger. But recently he had been on edge because he was working overtime. Papa was a building contractor, and he wanted to finish his latest job before they left for the big family reunion. This year it was going to be in Natchitoches, Louisiana, the place where Ray's Creole family began. His sister, Marguerite, was excited. She said it was going to be the best family reunion ever.

❀   ❀   ❀

By noon the next day, the pleasant coolness of the morning had gone. Now it was hot. Windows were open. The clatter of lunch dishes, sounds of piano lessons, and voices of neighbors spread through Ray's El Cerritos neighborhood in California.

Ray's friends were waiting for him to go back to the park. He was walking out the door when Marguerite reminded him, "Papa said for you to mow the lawn today."

"I know. I'll have time when I come back."

"It's already two o'clock. You've been gone all morning. Besides, I'm not cleaning up your mess in the kitchen."

"You're not my boss. You don't tell me what

to do." But Ray knew he had better do what she said. He called to his friends, "Go ahead. I'll meet you there later."

When he had finished doing the dishes, he started mowing the lawn. Heat beat down. As he pushed the mower, sweat poured off his face. Knowing he had to get the lawn in perfect shape before his papa got home, he dared not take a break.

When he had finished, the grass was smooth, emerald. Green. He looked around. That looks good, he thought, pleased with himself. He hoped his papa would be pleased, too. He thought of his friends, but it was late and he was too tired to go to the park.

He went to his room and threw his cap on a chair. Hot and sweaty, he decided to watch a video his father had bought him about a boy who lived in Haiti long ago, during the revolution there. He liked it because the boy was a hero and because his own ancestors had come from Haiti to Louisiana long ago. He lay on the cool floor, relaxed.

Just as he was settled, Marguerite disturbed

the quiet. "Ray, come see."

"I can't. I'm busy."

She came to his room. "You've seen that a million times. Turn it off and come help me."

In her room he found her trying on clothes. "What're you doing, girl?" She had clothes all over the place.

"I'm trying to decide what I'm gonna take to the reunion. Do you think I should wear this dress to the banquet? "

"Now don't ask me. That's up to you."

Suddenly the back door slammed, and Papa's voice rang out, "Ramon, Ramon! Come here, right now!" Ray had been named for his Great-gran-papa Ramon Baptiste Moret.

"When he calls you 'Ramon,' you are in trouble, *mo frèr*. What've you done now?"

"Don't call me *mo frèr*."

"You are my brother, are you not? And you had better learn how to say more than 'good morning' in our Creole language."

Ray didn't like her speaking Creole to him. He hurried to his papa.

"What did I ask you to have done when I got

4

home from work?"

"To mow the lawn. And I mowed it."

"Come. Look at this yard! Grass clippings everywhere—on the walk, in the driveway. Get this cleaned up right now."

Ray, surprised at his papa's tone, stood with his head down.

"Go on, get it up. When are you going to learn to do something right? You know, you just like your Gran-papa Philippe. Can't depend on you to do anything. You're just like him. Even look like him." With that he turned and walked away.

Ray's throat tightened and tears welled in his eyes as he swept the grass from the walk. Suddenly he was angry. Lately his papa seemed more disappointed than pleased with him. Can't do nothing right for him, he thought. He thrashed the grass, making it more difficult for himself.

His moman drove up from work. "What's wrong?"

Ray did not answer. He kept right on sweeping wildly.

"Whatever it is, you're doing a fine job on the lawn." She walked inside. Ray sighed deeply, glad she was leaving him alone.

2

Who Is This Gran-papa Philippe?

IN THE KITCHEN Marguerite could hardly keep her secret. "Guess what, Ray?" she said. "We got some unbelievable news today. Gran-papa Philippe is coming to the reunion."

"Why is that unbelievable? He's part of the family, isn't he?"

"Well, he hasn't been to reunions I've been to. We both know Papa never talks to him, and neither did Gran-moman Suzette. With them it was like he didn't exist."

Ray asked, "Are you glad Gran-papa

Philippe is coming?"

"I don't know. I don't know him, but yeah . . . I'm glad. I just hope Papa's glad."

"Glad about what?" Moman asked, coming into the kitchen.

"I was telling Ray about Gran-papa Philippe's coming to the reunion."

"And it's about time," Moman said.

"Why doesn't Gran-papa Philippe come?" Ray wanted to know.

"Now don't ask that question," Marguerite said.

"What is he like?" Ray asked.

"I don't know. I never met your gran-papa. And your gran-moman never spoke of him to me. Ms. Suzette married your Gran-papa Philippe when she was very young. Her family was well-to-do. They were builders like your papa's uncles. They built houses and did a lot of the ironwork in New Orleans."

"Gran-moman was sharp," Marguerite said. "Liked expensive things."

"Yeah, wore a hat and gloves every time she walked out of her door," Moman said. "She talked a lot, but she never said a word to me about your Gran-papa Philippe."

"I don't remember hearing about him at the reunions, either," Marguerite said.

"Yes, they say as little as possible about him. But it is rumored that he is one good-looking Moret." Moman laughed. "Of course, a lot of Morets are good-looking."

"I've heard so much about this reunion I can hardly wait, even though I won't know most of them," Ray said.

"Yes, we haven't been since you were five, Ray. You wouldn't remember much," Moman said.

"You'll like our cousins. They're so much fun, especially Antoinette and Mary Louise. Every letter and phone call now is about nothing but our getting together at the reunion."

"With Gran-papa Philippe there, this should be a good reunion," Ray said.

"Maybe, but I don't know how your papa is gonna take his coming," Moman said.

"We can't know how it's going to be. We don't know him," Marguerite said.

"Don't know who?" Papa asked, walking into the room.

"Louis, you won't believe this," Moman said. "I got a letter from Aunt Mary Thérèse. Your papa is coming to the reunion."

The way anger took over his papa's face surprised Ray. "I guess that's why he called here yesterday."

"What did he say?" Moman asked, surprised.

"You know I have nothing to say to that man, Cam. And if he's coming to the reunion, then we won't be going."

So that's who it was, Gran-papa Philippe! "Why you say we won't be going because he's coming?" Ray asked, still wondering why his papa was so angry on the phone.

"I don't have to say why. And don't you ask." His papa gave him a withering look.

"I know you don't mean that," Moman said. "You've looked forward to going to this reunion as much as anyone. So I know you won't let your papa's coming keep you from going."

"After all these years, why does he have to show now? Especially when we're going to the place that means so much to our family. By now he should know that the family can do very well without him."

"But Papa, why—"

Before Ray could finish, his papa looked at him and in a stern, cold voice said, "No 'But papa, why?' I don't know that man you call Gran-papa Philippe." He walked out of the room.

Marguerite turned on Ray. "You don't listen. Didn't we tell you, 'Don't ask'? No, you have to open your big mouth, 'But Papa, why?' You should've left it to Moman. Now we really might not go."

"Stop it, Marguerite," Moman said. "Ray has a right to ask. Now let's calm down and get ready for dinner."

The dinner hour was silent. Ray had no desire to eat. He still felt the hurt from the words of both Papa and Marguerite. After dinner Ray wanted to apologize to his papa, but when he looked into the office his papa was concentrating on building plans. Papa seemed too far away into his work to reach. Ray went to his room, wishing that he had someone to talk to. Someone who would say something, anything, about his Gran-papa Philippe.

He remembered a phone call soon after his gran-moman died. It was about two years ago. He had answered the phone and talked to this man.

"Who are you?" a deep voice had asked.

"I'm Ramon. Who's this?"

"Your Gran-papa Philippe. I'm glad to hear your voice, Ramon. I would say you are about nine years old, eh, a big boy, I take it."

"How did you know I'm nine?"

"Oh, I know about you, but not as much as I would like to know. I wish I had been there when you were born. Held you and saw your first smile. That would have been nice, ahn?"

Ray laughed. "I guess so."

"I really want to see you, Ramon."

"Call me Ray."

His papa came into the room and asked, "Who you talking to?"

When Ray had excitedly said, "This man says he's Gran-papa Philippe," his papa had snatched the phone and talked the way he talked the day before, then slammed down the phone. Why, Ramon thought. Why was his papa so angry with his own papa?

That night Ray stood in front of the mirror and looked carefully at his smooth, ebony, oval face. His round black eyes were shaded with long, curled lashes, and his straight black hair, cropped close, revealed a round, well-shaped head. He grimaced, showing the one dimple that also appeared when he smiled, revealing even white teeth. He was tall for his age, and he knew he was good at all the games he played—as good as or better than some of his friends. But he was worried.

Ray looked like nobody in his family that he knew. Not like his moman—she had thick, curly black hair and dark brown eyes with olive-toned skin. And certainly not like Marguerite and Papa, who both had light brown hair, light brown eyes, and light skin. He was much darker, much darker than all of them. He had always wondered where he came from.

He still looked at himself, letting his hand move along his chin and around his mouth. His papa stuck his head in the door and said, "Hey, you still searching for whiskers? Remember when I caught you trying to shave? You were just a little boy then."

Ray, surprised and pleased, laughed. "Yeah, I had lather all over my face and was just about to use the razor when you caught me, and said, 'Hey, what you doing? You have nothing there but skin. You don't shave skin.'" They both laughed.

Then Papa's mood changed suddenly and he said, "You'll probably never shave. You too much like your gran-papa. His skin was always smooth. He did not need to shave." With that he left the room.

Ray lay in bed, thinking, Who is this Gran-papa Philippe and what does he look like? He must look terrible, he thought. His papa seemed so angry and disappointed when he spoke of him with words filled with regret: "You just like your Gran-papa Philippe. Even look like him!" And tonight, "You'll probably never shave." Ray lay still and recalled the strong, warm voice on the phone of the man who wanted to meet him.

3

Reunion Plans

THE DAYS PASSED and the time to leave for the reunion was drawing close. Ray worried. He still didn't know if they were going or not. His papa hadn't mentioned it. Nobody said a word about it. Finally Ray said, "Moman, these are the only shoes I have, and they look pretty bad. I'll need some new ones if we're going to the reunion."

"You'll get some because we're going." She crossed her fingers and smiled at him.

"And you'll need a new cap," Marguerite

15

said. "That one you have will have to stay at home."

"No way. This cap goes where I go."

"Moman, tell him no way is he going to wear that cap. I don't want him embarrassing me."

"How can his wearing that cap embarrass you?" Moman asked.

"The thing I remember most about the last reunion is how they all looked at Ray."

"How did they look at me?" Ray asked.

"As if you were the most beautiful boy there," Moman said.

"Aw, Moman, you know. He has to look sharp."

"I don't have to *look* sharp. I *am* sharp."

"Tell her, Ray," Moman said.

"Moman, you always take Ray's side."

"Not always, only when he is telling the truth, Marguerite."

Ray looked at Marguerite and grinned. She said so that Moman could not hear, "Just wait till you get to Natchitoches, you'll see."

What will I see? he wanted to know. But her tone made him feel deep inside that it was something he dared not ask. When he was a little boy, walking home with his friend Mark, a girl was sharing candy. When she got to Mark, she said, "You can't have any 'cause you black." Then she gave Ray *two* pieces. Why? He had wanted to know, but never asked.

❖　　❖　　❖

On their way to the mall, Marguerite said, "I hope you don't let Ray pick cheap, ugly shoes. But I'll help him."

"No!" Ray said. "I don't need your help. Do I tell you what to buy?"

"No, I'm fifteen. I know what to buy," Marguerite bragged.

"All right, enough," Moman said. "You will go shopping for what you want, and I'll go with Ray to get his shoes. We'll meet you in the food court for lunch."

He wished he were shopping with Papa. There wasn't all the fuss. He could get a jacket, dress shoes, and sneakers in no time. "You like that jacket? Try it on. Try these shoes. You like 'em? Fine." Just like that and they were finished. But he hadn't shopped with Papa in a long time.

Now he had to go with Moman.

When they had left Marguerite, Ray thought about what Marguerite had said to him: "Just wait till you get to Natchitoches." Again he thought about the girl and the candy. He asked Moman, "You think I should get a new cap?"

"If you want it. Be nice. Yours is a little worn, and I'm sure it's sweaty." She laughed.

He loved his old cap. He wore it front, back, and sometimes on the side. "Maybe Marguerite is right."

"Right about what?" Moman asked. "Something's bothering you. What is it?"

"Oh, nothing. I was just thinking." He told Moman about the girl and the candy and what she had said. "Why did she say that Mark could not have some and I could?" he asked.

"She didn't know what *black* meant," Moman said. "She probably had heard somebody say that word about somebody they didn't like, and maybe she didn't like Mark but she liked you."

"I'll get a new cap." He looked at his mother and smiled.

❖   ❖   ❖

Marguerite was not in the food court when they arrived. They waited for what seemed to Ray a long time. Finally she came. "Let me see what you got. I hope they're not some cheap shoes. Can't you understand, I want you to look like a Moret, Ray."

"Please, Marguerite. Ray got what he wanted," Moman told her.

Marguerite looked in his bag and said, "Yes! And a cap!"

"And they were on sale," Moman said.

Later at dinner Papa asked, "What did y'all do today?"

"Ray got some new shoes and a new cap, thank goodness," Marguerite said. "And I shopped for some things for the reunion." She quickly left the table and came back. "I got this frame for our family picture for Great-gran-papa."

"Oh, Marguerite, that's lovely. Ray, what are you taking for Great-gran-papa's birthday?" Moman asked.

"I'll have something. A surprise," Ray answered.

"I said we're not going. I mean that," Papa said with quiet force.

There was silence. Ray looked at Marguerite and then at Moman, waiting to see what they would say. Moman said, "I think we need to discuss this, Louis."

"There's nothing to discuss," Papa said.

They ate in silence.

Finally Moman said, "There is a lot to discuss. I think you are being unfair, Louis. We've bought tickets, made hotel reservations. Are you just going to ignore that? Are you going to lose all that money?"

"I said we're not going. So there's nothing to discuss."

Ray felt uneasy, for he had never seen his papa so unwilling to talk things over.

"This reunion is the celebration of Great-gran-papa Ramon's ninetieth birthday," Moman said. "We need to go. They're only every three years. We missed the last one. Ray is now eleven. He needs to know the family. This time we're meeting in Natchitoches. And he needs to see the place where your family began."

"And this could be Great-gran-papa's last reunion," Marguerite said.

"Maybe this is something you and I have to settle, Cam," Papa said.

"No. This is about family, and our children are old enough to know why you are refusing to go. They should know everybody in the family who's willing to get together. They need to hear Great-gran-papa Ramon tell the story of their ancestors and how they came to live in this country. He is the best person I know to tell them."

"And he might not live much longer . . . ," Marguerite said.

"We know, we know," Ray said, and looked at his papa, surprised that he had opened his mouth.

Moman went on. "Your saying you won't go because your papa is coming makes no sense to me."

"It doesn't have to make sense to you. I know how he is. Listen, when I was Ray's age, I was in a school play. He promised to come. Did he come? No. Then everybody had two-wheelers. He promised me one. Did I get it? No.

Everybody worked hard, but all he wanted to do was his art. He promises his brothers he'll help them on a big job. He works for a few days, then he's off doing his thing. He makes all these promises, and you can't depend on him. I don't want to have anything to do with him. I'm not going anyplace where he is."

Ray felt weak in the stomach and tight in the chest. Maybe you can't depend on Gran-papa Philippe, Ray thought. "Maybe he won't come," he blurted out.

"Forget it, we're not going." When Papa said that, Ray just knew that it was final.

Moman steadied herself with her hands on the table and looked straight at Papa. "I have never gone against your wishes, Louis, never. But this time, I'm sorry. We are going with or without you. I hope it's with you."

Papa looked at Moman but said nothing. The quiet was tense, and Ray could hear his heart thumping.

"Please, Papa," Marguerite said. "We don't want to go without you. And like Ray said, he might not even come and then we would've missed it for nothing. "

"I just wish he would stay away. You think I don't want to be with the family? I want to see Uncle Dominique. He was like a father to me. I want to get some advice about this construction work I'm doing. They'll be proud to see what I'm doing. I'll have to think about it," Papa said.

The tension was relieved, and Ray felt like saying out loud, "Yes!" but he dared not celebrate too soon.

Late that night, when he couldn't sleep, he knocked lightly on Marguerite's door. "You 'sleep?"

"No. Come in. I can't sleep."

"Me neither. Think Papa's gonna go?"

"I don't know."

"What can we do?" Ray asked.

"Pack our things and think positive. I know you want to go because you've heard a lot about the family. It's nothing like being there. You'll see."

Early the next morning, Marguerite woke Ray. "Moman told me to wake you up. Papa is going!"

"He is?"

"Is that all you got to say? Boy, get out of that bed and jump up and down!"

Ray jumped out of bed, grabbed Marguerite, and twirled her around. "You said we were going, and you were right!"

4

Kouzens

THE AIRPLANE HAD climbed high above the clouds that looked like dirty wool. The clouds were thick and threatening. Marguerite and Papa sat together, and Ray sat beside his moman, reading. "Ray, look out the window. What's that below us?" Moman asked.

"Just clouds, Moman. We're way above them. So they're nothing to worry about."

Moman laughed. "I remember the first time you went to the reunion. We were flying above clouds. You looked out and said, alarmed,

'What's that?' I said, 'Clouds.' Ray, your eyes lit up and you became excited. You said, 'You know who's up here, don't you?'"

Ray's face burned, and he closed his book. Finally he said, "Maybe I thought we were in heaven then, but I know better now."

They changed planes in Dallas and took a very small plane. The loud, droning noise of the plane hurt Ray's ears, and the wavelike motion upset his stomach. He felt weak and nauseous. His mother showed him the bag to use if he got worse. Not nearly soon enough, they landed in a small airport about fifty miles from Natchitoches, Louisiana, the home of his papa's ancestors.

It was late afternoon when they arrived at the hotel. "This hotel is newer and much bigger, but not as nice as the one we were in before in New Orleans," Marguerite said.

Ray looked around and said, "It looks good to me."

The lobby was filled with people whose skin tones varied. Some were tan, olive, and light brown. But most of them were fair and looked very much like his papa and Marguerite. Everybody was hugging, backslapping, and laughing. Marguerite was greeted: *"Ma cherie, Marguerite, sa tchòb byen?"*

"Tant Thérèse! Byen. Et to?"

Ray looked at Marguerite and wondered, Who is this girl? She seemed at home at last with people who spoke her language freely. Marguerite was so excited, all over the place. It was *parkwa, mo cheri, ma cherie, tant,* and *nonk.*

Ray moved around, looking at everyone. He was looking for Gran-papa Philippe. Was Papa wrong? Did he really look just like Gran-papa? he wondered. In this range of color tones, everyone had skin lighter than his. He stood alone while Moman and Papa joined with the crowd, laughing. He had never seen them so excited, either. It was as if Papa had forgotten why he had been reluctant to come.

There were so many people. Most had driven to the reunion from places in Louisiana. Some were from Natchez, Mississippi, but none came from as far away as Ray's family. Some people there were much older than his moman and papa. Many were the same age as Marguerite. Some were his age, but he did not know anyone. Marguerite was so busy, surrounded by a group laughing and talking, that she forgot him until a boy about his age asked her, "Who's he?"

"Oh, *mo frèr*, Ramon," she said excitedly.

"*Te frèr?*" a girl asked, as if surprised that Ray could be Marguerite's brother.

"Yeah. *Mo frèr*. Come, Ray, *ta kouzin* Mary Louise." Mary Louise was one of Marguerite's favorites, but Mary Louise was cool toward Ray. Marguerite called other names that Ray knew he would have to try hard to remember. Then Marguerite introduced Ray to some of their uncles standing nearby. "Ray, *te Nonk Dominique et Nonk Antoine*." All the grown-ups were *nonk* and *tant* to all the children, even though some were really cousins, like Antoine was a cousin to Ray's Gran-papa Philippe.

"And who is Ray?" Nonk Dominique asked.

"I'm Ramon Moret."

"Oh, you're Louis's boy, of course. You have grown so much since last time."

As they were going back to the group, Ray

heard Uncle Dominique say, "How did I miss knowing him? He's just like that odd brother of mine, Philippe, Louis's papa."

Another girl and some boys had joined the crowd. Marguerite was very happy to see them, especially the girl, their cousin Antoinette, whom she had said Ray would like. Antoinette was very fair, with blue eyes and long, curly black hair. She was tall, thin, and glanced around as though she knew she was beautiful. She looked Ray up and down.

"I'm Ramon." Ray looked her in the eye.

She embraced him. *"Parkwa kouzen Ramon."* She introduced him to kouzen Jean-Paul, who was older than Ray, and to kouzen Joel Frederic, who was about Ray's age. Jean-Paul was tall, well built, and tan. He had lots of black hair and the beginnings of a thin black mustache. Joel was short and plump, with skin the color of honey. Ray liked the way Joel laughed, but he paid little attention to Ray and went on talking and laughing, getting reacquainted with Marguerite and the other cousins.

Finally Ray asked in a voice too loud, "Has

anybody seen my Gran-papa Philippe?"

His uncles nearby became silent. "He's not here, and we hope he won't come," Uncle Antoine said. "We don't need him here, looking like a street person with his black pouch and sandals." Everyone laughed.

Ray's face burned. He felt that he had asked the wrong question. And the look that Marguerite gave him let him know that he should have kept his mouth shut. He remembered what Uncle Dominique had said, "that odd brother of mine," and now this with Uncle Antoine. Why didn't they like his gran-papa?

Ray left the lobby and went to the room he shared with Marguerite to unpack his clothes. When everything was put away, he lay on the bed, feeling pretty much alone. Nobody had really noticed him, and his family was so busy with people they knew. Did they forget that he didn't really know those people and that those people didn't know him?

He thought of cousin Antoinette, who had introduced him to others. She looks white, he thought. And Mary Louise, who asked, *"Te frèr?"*

Was she surprised that I'm Marguerite's brother? he wondered. Antoinette really thinks she's pretty. But I guess she's nice.

He must have fallen asleep, for it was dark when Marguerite entered their room. "Where'd you run off to? I looked all over for you. More people came." She sat on his bed.

"Did Gran-papa Philippe come?"

"Not yet. And please don't go round asking people about him. I don't think people really know him."

"You mean you don't think people like him, eh?"

"That's not what I said."

"Hey, who is this cousin Antoinette?"

"She is Papa's Tant Mary Therèse's grand-daughter. Papa doesn't have any sisters or broth-ers. But we're lucky we have great-aunts and great-uncles on Papa's side, and lots of cousins."

"Antoinette must think she's all that."

"Not Antoinette. She's seventeen, and this will be her second year in college. I think she's pretty. It's her mother, our cousin Ramona, who thinks she's special. She won't be here. She passes."

"What you mean, passes?"

"Ray, where have you been all of your eleven years? She's white."

"How can she be white? Why would she wanna be white?"

"Some do it just to get better jobs, and to go places where white people don't want us to go. And some do it because they wanna be white. But it's mostly to get good jobs. She had a tight job in a bank and worked there until she left for a better job and got away with it."

"Is Antoinette white?"

"Naw, silly. She could pass, though, easily, but I don't think she would."

"Would you?"

"Maybe. If I really thought it was profitable."

"That's ill. I'd never do something like that," Ray said.

"Naw, you couldn't even if you wanted to," she said angrily, and left the room.

His face burned. Had he hurt her by saying that to want to pass was ill?

He ran after her. "Marguerite, Marguerite, come back." She kept going. He knew by the tone of her voice she had meant to hurt him. And she had.

◈　　◈　　◈

Just as he finished dressing for dinner, there was a light knock on the door. "Ray, are you ready?" It was his moman.

"Come in," Ray called.

"How is it going? Are you having a good time?"

"I guess. Everybody here is so different. Most of them are like Marguerite and Papa. Why am I not like you and them?"

She looked at him, and he was sorry that he had asked. She smiled. "That's a hard question to answer, but I'll try. There are so many things that make us who we are. First it's family, and family goes way back. We don't know all of the peoples who share in the making of us. But that's why we're here at the reunion. We want you to learn more about the family. Ray, we are Creoles. That means we have West African, French, American Indian, and Spanish peoples in your papa's and my families. From all of these peoples, we get what makes us who we are. We get

33

skin color, hair and eye color, whether our hair is straight or curly, and how we look."

"Then why don't I look like you, Marguerite, and Papa?"

"You got skin color from the West African members of the family. I got my curly hair from my West African ancestors. You got your straight hair from the American Indian members; Marguerite and Papa got their hair and eyes and skin color from the French side. Yet we are one family. But individually we are all different. There is no one like you, Ray. We cannot control our beginnings and our endings, but what we are in between is left up to us. I'm so proud that you are creating a beautiful person who I call my son."

Ray looked at her and smiled. There was silence between them. Finally she asked, "Does that answer your question?"

"Yes, Moman." He was pleased with "creating a beautiful person." Still smiling, he said, "I'm hungry. Let's eat."

At dinner Ray was unusually quiet. "What happened with you, Ray?" Papa asked. "Great-gran-papa was in the lobby for a little while. He asked for his namesake. You were nowhere to be found."

"He was in the room feeling sorry for himself," Marguerite said.

"Ray is finding his way about just fine, aren't you, Ray?" Moman said.

"Yeah."

They talked about a lot of people there, but not a word was said about Gran-papa Philippe. Ray wanted to ask a million questions. Why didn't people like Gran-papa Philippe? Were more people coming? And would any of them look more like him? But having been stung so many times within a few hours, he remained quiet.

Later that night, when he was settled in his bed, he was still feeling hurt about what he had said to Marguerite about passing and what she had said to him. "Marguerite, about that passing stuff. I—"

Before he could finish, Marguerite said angrily, "Forget it. Good-night."

He lay still, thinking of what had happened

since they arrived. Was Marguerite ashamed of him? And cousin Mary Louise, who was surprised that he was a part of the family? He thought of Joel's laughter and of Antoinette, who alone out of all of them had greeted and welcomed him and introduced him to others.

5

Sugarcane Surprise

RAY AWOKE EARLY. He dressed quickly and quietly and went down to the lobby. He wanted to know if his gran-papa had arrived in the night. How could he find out? There was no one in the lobby except a young man behind the registration desk. *"Bon maten,"* he said to Ray.

Ray smiled. *"Bon maten."* He was so glad that he knew how to say 'good morning' in Creole.

"How can I help you?"

"I stay here, and I'm waiting for somebody."

"Is that person here with us?"

"I don't know, and I don't know how to find out."

"What's the name?"

"Philippe Moret."

The man looked. "We have many Morets, but no Philippe."

Disappointed, Ray walked outside of the hotel. *Gran-papa has to come today. Tonight is the big celebration of Great-gran-papa's birthday. Everyone will have arrived and will be in a good mood. There will be plenty of food and music and dancing. He had better come,* Ray said to himself.

When he went back inside, there was a tall woman who was very fair with hazel eyes and graying hair talking to the uncles that Ray had met. When she saw Ray, she said, "Oh, *bon maten, mo cheri.*"

"*Bon maten.*" Ray smiled.

He wanted to know who she was, but she kept right on talking. "I don't care, *sa mo frèr,* and that I cannot ignore."

"*Sa mo frèr, tro,*" Dominique said.

"And *mo kouzen,*" Antoine said. "But that's no

reason why we should ignore how awful he is. I thought he would give up that painting, a *black Christ*, for heaven sakes."

"Aw, Antoine, that was eons ago; he was just a boy," the woman said. "And I think your attitude about that subject is very old-fashioned."

"But it's not just that," Nonk Dominique said. "He is still against everything we believe in. We are good Catholics. And does he believe in working like the rest of us? No."

"He works! At what he likes. He may not be as wealthy as you, but he makes a living," the woman said. "I hope he comes."'

Were they talking about his gran-papa? Ray wondered. He wanted to interrupt but decided to go back to the room and wait for his family. When they came down for breakfast, the lobby was filled with people. Ray looked for Jean-Paul and Antoinette. They were not there. Then he saw the woman who had spoken to him. She was alone. He turned to Marguerite. "Who's that lady?"

"That's our Tant Thérèse, Antoinette's gran-moman. Come. Tant Thérèse, this is Ramon."

"I know. When I saw you this morning, my heart stopped. I wanted to do this." She grabbed Ramon and folded him in her arms. Then she held him at arm's length. "You are so much like my missing brother. You look just like him. But Antoine and Dominique"—she beat the air with one hand—"they would not have understood."

"Is he coming?" Ray asked.

"Who knows? We will only know when we see him. I'm sure you've noticed that you get nowhere asking questions about him. But I want you to know that he has always been my favorite brother, even if he is out of step with most of us." She laughed, left them, and was soon surrounded by others.

"She likes Gran-papa Philippe," Ray said.

"Yeah," Marguerite said. "Now all you need to do is what we told you before we left home. Don't ask."

❖　❖　❖

For the big celebration of Great-gran-papa's birthday, each child was to bring a small gift—something that would add to or spark discussion on the life and history of the family. Marguerite had reminded Ray, but he arrived with no gift. He didn't know what to bring to the celebration that night. When they went shopping, he saw some stalks in a barrel about two inches around with joints that were equally spaced. The stalks were purple streaked with green. "What's that?" he asked Papa.

"Sugarcane. Remember I told you that your Great-great-gran-moman Claudia Moret raised lots of sugarcane that helped the family survive. This is it."

"Oh, yeah, a long, long time ago. I think I'll give Great-gran-papa a gift of sugarcane." He selected a short stalk.

"Is that your big surprise?" Marguerite asked. "Ray, that's no gift. Can't you find something else?" She had spent a lot of time putting the picture in her frame for her gift. "You shouldn't wait till the last minute."

"Ray, let's look around," Moman said.

"No, this is what I want to give when I say happy birthday to Great-gran-papa."

That evening everyone was dressed up. The women wore summer dresses with high-heeled sandals. And even though it was hot and humid, the men had on suits and ties. Jewelry sparkled. Yet everyone was relaxed. There was lots of talk and laughter. Great-gran-papa came into the lobby, and there was a great stir. Everyone wanted to say hello to him. He was not a tall man. He looked as if at one time he had been stocky. His skin was fair, like most of the family's. He had broad facial features, and his white hair was fine and thinning.

While they were waiting for everyone to assemble to go together into the room where the celebration would be held, Great-gran-papa was seated. He sat looking around the room. His bright, dark eyes were sharp, and he wore no glasses. Was he, too, looking for his son Gran-papa Philippe? Ray wondered.

Ray moved about the room, darting in and out of groups that were laughing and talking, having a great time. Where was his gran-papa? Was he coming? Soon they would be going to the place where the celebration would be held. Why didn't he come? Ray knew that he would soon have to join his family to go to the celebration.

He didn't want to leave the hotel lobby. What if Gran-papa came? He would not know where to go.

Ray decided to walk once more to the front of the lobby. Just as he got near the door, a tall, ebony man with dark eyes walked in. His hair was long and straight with streaks of gray. He was dressed in jeans ironed with creases. He wore a soft denim shirt buttoned at the neck with no tie. And he wore a dark blue linen jacket and expensive leather sandals. He carried a black pouch that hung from a shoulder strap. He looked cool on that hot summer night. Seeing him, Ray knew immediately that it was Gran-papa Philippe.

"You've come. I knew you would come," Ray said, running toward him.

"Yes, I'm here. And you are?"

"Ramon. Ramon Baptiste Moret!"

"You are me with my papa's name!"

Ray hugged him around the waist and hid his face in the hard stomach of the man whom he looked so much like.

Proudly but afraid of what his papa would

say, Ray walked hand in hand with his gran-papa. Everyone was getting ready to go into the banquet hall. The lobby became quiet as Gran-papa walked up to his papa. "It's been a long time. I am glad to be home."

Great-gran-papa embraced his son and said with a strong, clear voice, "Now the celebration can begin."

As Tant Thérèse and a few others came over to greet Gran-papa Philippe, Ray left him. He joined his family and went into the room where the celebration was to be held.

The look on his papa's face let Ray know that he was not at all pleased. Over the voice of Tant Thérèse, who was welcoming the crowd and get-ting things under way, Ray said to him, "He's here!"

"I know," Papa said in a voice that expressed his anger. "And I'm telling you now I don't want you hanging around him."

"Louis, please, don't. Let the children have a great time," his moman said.

When everyone had settled into the room, Tant Thérèse called for their attention. "This is the biggest reunion yet. Have you ever seen so many Morets, Baptistes, and Radcliffs in one place? We have come to honor our ancestors and pay homage to Great-gran-papa Ramon Baptiste. I want all of you to know that I insisted on my brother Philippe being here. I am glad that he has come." There was sparse applause.

"Most people feel like me. He shouldn't have come," Papa said.

Tant Thérèse went on. "So now the children will introduce themselves and give Great-gran-papa their gifts." The children lined up, the youngest ones up front.

Ray stood in line between his cousins Joel and Jean-Paul and watched as the younger children gave their gifts. One little girl, wishing him happy birthday, said, *"Bon année*, Great-gran-papa Ramon."* And everyone applauded. Some said, *"Felicitation"* or *"Bon sante*, Great-gran-papa."* Greetings and a wish for good health were said by many. There was a great variety of gifts: maps of old Louisiana, Saint Domingue, old Haiti, and the old city of Le Cap; and lots of pictures of families framed the way Marguerite had done hers.

Ray looked at his gift and wondered if he had made a good choice. He stepped out of the line. He didn't know what he would say. But what would his moman and papa think if he didn't give a present? And Great-gran-papa and Gran-papa Philippe?

When Marguerite gave her gift, there was applause. Ray did not look at his parents, but he knew they were pleased. Only three people were waiting when Ray stepped back in line. Finally it was his turn. He walked up to his great-gran-papa and introduced himself. "Great-gran-papa, I have your name and the looks of your son Philippe." There was a heavy silence in the room. "I have brought to you sugarcane, the crop that Great-great-gran-moman Claudia Rocque Moret raised to help our family survive. Happy ninetieth birthday." There was silence still. Then there was great applause.

Great-gran-papa gave Ray a hug and said, "My moman would be proud to know that Ramon Baptiste Moret II still pays homage to sugarcane. I know the ancestors are pleased that we have so many wonderful children to carry on our names. Children, stand and take your bows." There was loud applause. Then the real festival of food, music, and dance began.

6

The Two Meet Again

EARLY THE NEXT MORNING, Ray checked the schedule to see what was happening that day. He noticed that there would be a boat ride on Cane River Lake and a picnic and games at a park in the city. Then in the evening, Great-granpapa would tell the story of the family's coming to Louisiana from Haiti.

While the halls in the hotel were quiet and Marguerite was in deep sleep, Ray dressed and went into the lobby. There were people arriving, but they didn't look like members of his family.

He was beginning to see how much his family looked alike. He walked outside. The weather was hot and humid, even that early.

Feathery clouds glowed pink from the sun that was still young on the horizon. He walked to the back of the hotel and saw dark water flowing swiftly by. He stood listening. The water, as dark as red wine, hardly made a sound as it rushed on its way. Suddenly he felt a hand on his shoulder. He looked up, and there was Gran-papa Philippe. He was carrying the black pouch.

"You always such a early riser, ahn?" Gran-papa asked.

"No, sir," Ray answered with a feeling of awe.

"I don't get much sleep, now. 'Tis good to see someone else up early. I am so glad it's you."

"I'm glad, too." Ray waited to see what would follow. They stood silent and watched the water flow on its way.

Two boys in a small canoe paddled down the river, making waves that lapped the shore.

"Long time ago this river was called the Red River," Gran-papa finally said.

"What is it called now?"

"Cane River Lake, and if we follow it up a little way we'll come to the place built by one of our ancestors, Mary Thérèse Unwa."

"Unwa? Is that a French name?"

"No."

"Papa always says our ancestors were French."

"Unwa's papa was an African slave who belonged to a Frenchman, commander of the French post named for the Natchitoches Native Americans. His Christian name was François. He married a young African woman whose African name was Ngozi.

"Where were they from?"

"They were from Nigeria. An Ibibio tribe there has that word *unwa*, which means "second daughter." François and Mary François's second daughter was named Unwa. And four of their eleven children had African names, also."

"Did they speak an African language?"

"Yes, they were fortunate. They spoke their language. It is believed that the language we speak today, Creole, is greatly influenced by the language the Africans spoke here in Louisiana. Fortunately there was a law then that did not let slave owners sell husbands and wives and children away from one another. Come, we can go now to the place Unwa built."

Ray noticed that the sun was now up on the horizon and that people were about. "I had better get back. Maybe later."

"But there is the boat ride," Gran-papa said.

"I won't go, maybe. I'll meet you here when they have all gone."

When he had left Gran-papa, he wondered why he had promised to come back. His papa had told him to stay away from Gran-papa. But he wanted to go see that place. Ray found his family in the hotel restaurant.

"Where were you, Ray?" his papa asked. "You're exploring?"

"There's a river in back there. I went to see it. Gran-papa was walking there, and—"

"I told you I don't want you around that man," Ray was interrupted angrily.

"I didn't go with him; he was just there."

"Well, just don't go seeking him out. Hurry

now and get something to eat. We're going down that river on the boat ride. I want you to get to know your Nonk Dominique, the man who was really my papa. This trip will be a good time."

Ray knew that if he asked not to go now, he would have to find a good excuse. He wanted to go with Gran-papa. What could he do? He remembered that he had been sick on the plane. "My stomach is not right yet, from when I was sick on the plane. Maybe I shouldn't go. I don't want to be sick for the picnic."

"I don't know about you staying here alone," Papa said.

"That boat ride might make him feel worse," said Moman.

"I'll stay with him," Marguerite volunteered.

Oh, no, Ray thought. I'd rather go. But before he could protest, Moman said, "Oh, no, you will not. Ray will be fine. Where can he go except around this hotel? There is a lot of family here to see that he's okay."

Ray was so happy he wanted to give his moman a big hug. But he remained calm and said, "I don't feel like eating much. Just some juice, and maybe some cereal."

When his family was about to leave, Marguerite said, "You sure you don't feel like going, Ray? I don't think you'll be happy here by yourself."

"He'll be all right," Moman said.

Ray was so relieved he gave Moman a brief hug and waved good-bye to them. He now wished he had eaten a big breakfast before saying that his stomach was upset!

7

Indigo Plantation

AFTER EVERYONE WHO was going on the boat ride had left, Ray rushed down to the bank of the river. Gran-papa Philippe was not there, but Antoinette was a distance away, walking toward him.

"*Bon maten*," she called out to him.

Ray waved to her. "*Bon maten, ma cherie.*"

"*Bon! Bon!*" She laughed excitedly. "So *vou parle kréyol*, ahn, Ramon?"

"Oh, a little. You can call me Ray."

"What are you doing down here?"

"Aw, nothing." He dared not tell her he was waiting for someone. He wanted her to be gone before Gran-papa got there.

"I know there is a place up there somewhere that once belonged to our ancestors. I couldn't find it. I probably didn't go far enough. I'd like to. I'm for knowing as much as I can about my African people."

"You? But you could . . . er . . . what's that word? Like, be white."

"Pass. My mother passes, but I wouldn't. Gran-moman tells me about how our ancestors from Africa struggled here in this place to give us a good life. They made this family what it is. I'm okay with the African in me."

"Gran-papa Philippe was telling me about Unwa." Suddenly he became afraid. What if she told Marguerite? He would be in trouble. But Antoinette was not interested in Unwa.

"You can see they don't like my Nonk Philippe. And they don't care much for people who like him."

"Why?"

"He's different. They won't admit that he is

good-looking and that he's good at anything he does. He could be as well off as the rest of the brothers and cousins if he wanted to build things. He's the best at cabinetmaking, but he prefers to paint and write. He's good at that, too. He's just plain smart."

"I don't know him."

"I don't want you to go against your papa, but you get to know your gran-papa. I guess besides me, my gran-moman is the only one here who really likes him. She says he is misunderstood, but sometimes you can't depend on him. But I like him, and I like you. You're good-looking like him. While he's here, you be smart and find a way to get to know him." She paused. "Are you going back to the hotel now?"

"No, I am going to stay here awhile," Ray said.

"I'll see you later."

Ray wanted to ask her to stay and go up the river to that place with them. He liked her, but he wasn't sure. She might tell Marguerite that he was with Gran-papa. He waited alone. He waited and waited. Maybe Gran-papa had forgotten that they had planned to go. It was getting very hot, and the humid air made Ray feel tired. He wished his gran-papa would come. He thought about Antoinette's words: "They don't like him. He's different. Sometimes you can't depend on him." It was what Papa said. He wished he'd gone on the boat ride. Just as he was about to go back to the hotel, Gran-papa arrived, carrying the black pouch. Ray wondered what was in it.

"What took you so long? I thought you forgot," Ray said.

"I can see that you're impatient. Time is a tortoise when you're young. At my age time has become the hare. I am here; let's be on our way."

Ray tried to keep from laughing. Tortoise and the hare, he's funny, he thought. Ray did not have to slow his pace to keep up with Gran-papa, who moved with a steady rhythm. There was so much he wanted to say to his gran-papa. Where did he live? What did he do when he was a boy? But the words just wouldn't come. The silence remained between them.

Along the way Ray saw beautiful green trees and trees with limbs bleached white by the sun.

The trees were covered with silver gray moss hanging almost into the water. The moss was like ghosts among the lush trees and brush near the bank of Cane River Lake.

"Look at that. Is that gray stuff some kind of parasite?"

"No. What you see is life on death. Those white trees are very dead. The moss, very much alive, has a life of its own."

In spite of the strange beauty near the dark water, Ray was worried as they walked along its bank. Suppose that boat with his parents came by? He would really be in trouble. But pretty soon they went inland.

They did not talk again until they walked along under trees loaded with pecan nuts. Nuts were scattered on the ground. "These are delicious. Let's have some," Gran-papa said.

"But we don't have a nutcracker."

"Oh, but we do," Gran-papa said.

"No, no-oo, not my teeth," Ray said, laughing.

"What was man's first tool?" Gran-papa asked.

"I don't know. Maybe the wheel?"

"Oh, no, the wheel came much later. A nutcracker."

"Aw, you kidding me."

"Oh, I'm very serious." Gran-papa picked up two nuts and placed them together in the palm of his hand. He squeezed them until they cracked apart. "See, man's first tool was his hand, and that's a nutcracker."

"Wow! I never would have guessed that." The nuts were rich and sweet. They walked on past a field gleaming white in the late morning sun.

"Know what that is?" Gran-papa asked.

"Yes, but I didn't know it was that beautiful," Ray said.

"Cotton is a pleasant sight this time of year if you don't have to pick it. Unwa with her children never grew much cotton. Indigo, tobacco, and cattle made their fortune. Oh, yes, she was quite a woman. Produced quite a clan."

"Did you know her?" Ray asked.

"I'm pretty old, but not that old. Unwa was seventeen in 1760. Some say that Unwa saved her mistress's life and was freed from slavery. Others say something else."

"What do others say?"

"I'm not sure a boy so young will understand all that happened in the lives of African people back then."

"I'll understand. Tell me, what do others say?"

"When Unwa was twenty-five, a young Frenchman, named Claude Pierre Conant, came to Natchitoches. I shall call him Pierre."

"This place?"

"Oh, no. Natchitoches then was just a little outpost for the French. A military post. There was a lot of land and few people. With the coming of Pierre, Mary Thérèse Unwa's life changed."

"How did he change Unwa?"

"There were so few people on the post, he could not help knowing her."

"Was she pretty?"

"There're no pictures. But word is that she was attractive. She was black. Like me and you." He looked down on Ray, placed a hand on his shoulder. Ray looked up, their eyes caught, and they smiled.

"But I guess back then they didn't have makeup, soaps, creams, and stuff like that, eh? " Ray said.

"No, you're right. But she was a strong personality, Unwa, and smart, too. Maybe I should let my sister tell you this story."

"Why? I bet she doesn't know it as good as you. Tell me."

"Anyway, this young Frenchman Pierre paid Unwa's owner a sum, and Unwa went to work for him for a place in his house with room and board."

"He could really do that?"

"It was against the law, but the commander of the post was a relative of the owner, so the law was ignored.

"She lived with him many years, and they had ten children—the first Creoles of African descent in the Cane River area. All that time she and the children still belonged to the mistress who let her go live with Pierre."

"His children were slaves?"

"Yes, their children belonged to her mistress. That was the law. Finally Pierre purchased her and the children."

"Then they were free."

"No, they were still his slaves."

"Wow! That's not true."

"We have the records. He freed Unwa, but not the children until they were much older. She had nothing when she became free. No land, no money. However, when he freed them, he gave each son a little less than five acres of land, and he put her in charge of it.

"She and the sons worked to clear the land of yucca plants and cypress trees. With the trees they built houses, and on the cleared land they planted tobacco. With money that they got from tobacco, indigo dyes, bear skins, and bear grease, they bought cattle. They saved their money and bought more land."

In the distance Ray saw what to him looked like the steeple of a church. "Is that a church?" he asked Gran-papa.

"It is. Your ancestors were very devout Catholics. In 1829 they built what may be the oldest church by and for free people of color in this country."

Just then, beyond a stand of trees, Ray saw a big white house. "We're here," Gran-papa said. "That's Indigo Plantation, now a historic site. Your ancestors built this place. Unwa lived there. They called it Honeysuckle."

"That's a nice name," Ray said. "But why Honeysuckle?"

"Once there used to be a lot of plants all over that had small white flowers with sweet nectar. When Unwa built here, she named the place after that plant."

"They must have had a lot of money to get that much land."

"At that time in 1800, the French and Spanish governments, wanting people to settle in Louisiana, gave people land. This was called a land grant. Unwa and her sons received grants, and they also bought land. By 1810 they had more than twelve thousand acres of land."

"Unwa and her children worked that land alone?" Ray asked.

"No. They purchased their relatives who

were enslaved and other slaves to help them establish a wealthy homestead for themselves."

"Papa never said we had that much land."

"We don't."

"Who owns it now?"

"I don't know. But the last owner named it Indigo."

"Why did our ancestors sell it?" Ray asked.

"They didn't sell it. It was stolen from them after France sold Louisiana to the United States. Under the French, Creoles and free African people did very well. Under the United States, any people with African blood were treated all the same. Even the free ones were treated as slaves. The very well-to-do children of Pierre and Unwa were no longer respected as landowners. They lost a lot."

"Can we go onto the grounds and inside?"

"Sure. No guards are here, ever. The grounds are always open to the public. But sometimes when they expect lots of visitors, they use guides. There're some interesting things I want to show you, but we had better get back to the hotel. There's a lot planned for today."

"But tell me—"

"No more today. Meet me early in the morning and we'll see Honeysuckle."

All of a sudden heavy, dark clouds threatened above, and thunder rumbled in the distance. The river seemed restless as the dark water churned into white foam. Ray and Granpapa hurried along, Ray hoping that it would not rain before they reached the hotel. In spite of the clouds, it was still stifling hot. Sweat poured off Ray, but the heat didn't seem to bother Granpapa Philippe.

Lightning flashed, and the thunder clapped overhead. Suddenly huge drops of rain splattered here and there. Just as they reached the hotel, the clouds opened and a downpour of rain had them scrambling inside. Ray sat with his gran-papa by a window and looked out at the rain, wondering if his family was still on the boat.

"We won't have a picnic now," Ray said.

"That's a Louisiana squall. It will end as quickly as it has come," Gran-papa said.

The gray rain fell heavily upon the window

and made Ray sleepy. He did not want to leave Gran-papa Philippe. But he was afraid that his papa would enter the lobby and see them together. He said to his gran-papa, "It'll have to be early in the morning when we go. I'll see you then." He went to the room and lay upon the bed and fell fast asleep.

❀   ❀   ❀

Marguerite woke him. "Get up, the sun is shining after all that rain. The picnic is still on, so get up."

Ray felt like staying in bed, but he was so hungry he knew he was going to the picnic, where there would be lots of food, a lot to drink, and music and games.

"You missed it, Ray. That river lake is so beautiful. You should have seen the trees with all that moss. It was weird."

Ray wished he could tell her that he saw the trees and lots more with Gran-papa Philippe. But he let her rave on while he pretended great interest, sometimes saying with regret in his voice, "Aw, I wish my stomach wasn't acting up.

Was it weird like ghosts?"

"Yes, exactly! How'd you know?"

"I'm not without a brain, you know." Ray looked at her and grinned.

8

Family Tug o' War

RAY CAME OUT READY for the picnic with his new cap turned backward. They were waiting for their papa when Marguerite said, "Ray, where you think you're going looking like that?"

"Looking like what? Nothing's wrong with me."

"Moman," Marguerite said. "Tell him to turn that cap around. Why does he always have to dress like that? He's different enough."

"Marguerite, why are you so worried about Ray? You insisted on his getting a new cap.

Now you worried because it's on backward. Nothing's wrong with him wearing his cap like that."

"It is, too. Nobody here is wearing a cap backward."

"I don't see nobody here wearing a cap," Ray said, and laughed.

Marguerite said angrily, "Then why do you? You stand out enough."

Ray looked at his moman, turned his cap around, and lowered his head.

"Turn your cap back around, Ray," Moman said. "I'm sure if the other boys had on caps, some of them would be turned backward. And Marguerite, I want you to leave Ray alone."

The family had a large space reserved in the park, and many of them were already there when Ray's family arrived. Ray looked around for Gran-papa, but he did not see him. What would Ray do if he saw him there? And would Gran-papa speak to them? Ray was worried and afraid that Papa might be rude and hurt Gran-papa's feelings.

In spite of the rain, it was now sunny and

very hot. Tables were filled with crawfish, bisque, shrimps, sausages, baguettes stuffed with fried fish, and oysters. There were potato salads, vegetable salads, and fruits. There were also greens, string beans, and huge pots of Creole gumbo and rice. The dessert table was filled with apple, peach, and lemon tarts, sweet potato pie, pecan pie, and cakes with coconut and pecan icings. Having had only juice and a little cereal all day, Ray's stomach growled with hunger.

He eagerly filled a plate and was on his way to sit with his papa when Gran-papa hailed him. "Ramon." When he came nearer, he said, "I like that cap. Oh, my, what a plate, my man. *Bon appétit*."

Before Ray could answer, his papa was there in Gran-papa's face. He lifted a hand and pointed a finger. "Stay away from my son. I mean it. Stay away, you hear?" He had not raised his voice, but the heat of his anger was there in his tense body. He took Ray roughly by the arm and led him to a table. Ray looked back, and Gran-papa was walking away.

Ray stood with the plate in his hand. He wanted to call out, "Gran-papa, I want to be with you," but he was still and silent. It was as if all life had gone out of him.

"Sit down and eat your food," his papa said.

Ray felt as though the heat of the sun was unbearable. Suddenly his stomach felt full but weak, and he was glad that there was nothing in it to come up. "I'm not hungry." He put the plate on the table and ran as fast as he could, not knowing where he was going, to get far away from his papa.

Marguerite and Antoinette were on the far side of the park and hailed him. "Ray, Ray," Marguerite called. Ray kept on running. They ran after him. Finally he stopped and sat at a table far from the family.

"Now what?" Marguerite asked, concerned.

"Gran-papa . . . ," and he burst into tears.

"Did you talk to him in front of Papa?"

"No."

"Then what did you do?"

"Nonk Philippe talked to him, that's what. He wants to know Ray," Antoinette said.

"But why can't he talk to us? He's our gran-papa," Marguerite said.

"Why can't he talk to anybody? You know, he doesn't live too far from Gran-moman and me, but we don't see him often. He's always been on the outs. He's too what they call Afrocentric. He's proud of his African ancestors. And he's a free spirit. People don't like it when you are not in step with them. That's a threat."

Ray sat listening to them. He was so ashamed. Why hadn't he run after Gran-papa?

"Ray, you know how Papa feels. And last night you were hand in hand with Gran-papa. I was glad there was no scene then. I want to get to know Gran-papa, too, but I don't want trouble here. Why can't you do what you're told?"

Ray was afraid that Antoinette was going to tell that she saw him by the river. "I don't go after him."

"Don't be upset, Ray, please. I think you'll get to know your gran-papa," Antoinette said.

"How can I? Nobody wants to talk about him."

"He's here, and you're ready. You two will

find a way. What you bet," Antoinette said. "Let's go. I know you're hungry, Ray."

"I'm not. And I want to stay here by myself."

They had not been gone long before his papa found him. "I brought your food, and I want you to eat. It's not you, Ray, and I'm not mad at you. But I want you to promise me you won't see him."

"I can't promise that. He's here. So what can I do?"

"You ignore him, and I'll take care of the rest."

"What's wrong with him? Why don't you like him, Papa?"

"I don't want to talk about it. Just stay away from him." His papa put an arm around his shoulder and they sat together, not talking. Ray sat, still feeling ashamed that he had not let Gran-papa know that he wanted to be with him. Finally he ate.

More people had arrived. Games were getting under way. Nonk Dominique was in charge of the tug o' war between families: the Radcliffs against the Baptistes, and the winner would take on the Morets. Ray was excited. Their cousins Jean-Paul and Mary Louise were Baptistes; Mary Ann and Antoinette were Radcliffs. Jean-Paul looks like a good athlete, Ray thought. Although a lot of Baptistes were tall and strong, Ray decided to root for the Radcliffs. Besides his liking Antoinette, if the Radcliffs won the Morets would have a better chance.

Of course, Antoinette had decided to stay on the sidelines with Marguerite so they could root for their special teams.

Marguerite was pulling for the Baptistes. "Why're you pulling for them?" Ray asked.

"They look like they'll win," Marguerite said.

"Yeah, and besides rooting for my favorite cousin's team, we'll probably lose if we have to go against the Baptistes," Ray said.

"Oh, you're so smart. Marguerite, let's listen to your brother and root for us Radcliffs."

"Not me. I'm still pulling for the Baptistes."

"I'm with you, Ray, of course. What's with your sister?" Antoinette asked.

"She's mad at me."

"Why is she mad at you?"

"Take a look at him," Marguerite said with disgust. "Cap on backward."

"He's cute," Antoinette said.

"Cute? He should be shading his face so he won't get any blacker from the sun," Marguerite said.

Ray's face burned, and it was hard for him to breathe. So that's it, he thought. It's not the cap, it's me. My being black, that's the difference that's bothering her.

"Marguerite!" Antoinette exploded. "If you think that about your brother, what do you think about my blue eyes?"

"I don't think about your blue eyes."

"Well, if you don't, a lot of people in this family do. Ray and Nonk Philippe are too black and I'm too white. Oh, yeah, they think about it. My gran-moman wants me darker; my moman wants me whiter. And everybody has to pass the paper bag test to really be accepted. But I'm surprised at you, Marguerite. I thought you loved your brother."

"I do. I love you, Ray," she cried. "Why do you think I want you to always look sharp? I know what people say about dark-skinned people. I'm trying to protect you."

"I know you love me," Ray said. They were quiet. Then suddenly he asked, "What's the paper bag test?"

Antoinette laughed. "Haven't you heard? The paper bag is light brown. Anything darker than that is really not tight in our world."

"It certainly is easier everywhere when you pass that test. I'm glad I pass it," Marguerite said.

"Well!" Antoinette looked at Ray. "We're different, eh, Ray?" Antoinette said. *"Vive la différence."*

Ray sat with his head down. He knew that his sister loved him. Now he also knew that she picked at him because she was ashamed of him. It really showed here at the reunion.

They had missed the tug o' war. The Baptistes had won.

Ray was pleased that his papa was pulling behind him in the Morets' line. There were so many of them that the Baptistes protested. Some had to sit down. The tug was on. Backward and forward they moved toward the line. Joel was right in front of Ray. Moman was on the sideline with the other Morets shouting, "Pull, pull!" The Radcliffs had tired the Baptistes. The Morets won!

Nonk Antoine was in charge of the three-legged sack race and the beanbag toss. For the sack race, he placed Ray with Cousin Augustine. Augustine was just a bit younger than Ray. He was small, sandy haired, and wore glasses. Ray was not so happy with the choice. He would have preferred Jean-Paul. Jean-Paul was placed with another cousin his size. The race was on. To Ray's surprise, Augustine was fast and could hop and step with him. They came in second, with Jean-Paul's team first.

There was much excitement at the beanbag toss. One would have five throws to place the beanbag through the hole in a board that had four holes. The holes varied in size. If you threw the beanbag in the biggest hole, you scored five points. In the smallest hole, you scored twenty points. Jean-Paul was in the lead with twenty-five points. When it became Ray's turn, Ray easily scored in the ten-point hole on the first try. He tried for fifteen points and missed. He tried again and the beanbag almost went in, but hung on the edge.

Papa groaned. Moman said, "Come on, Ray, you can do it." He only had two more tries. If he were to win, he would have to make the smallest hole. He tossed. It almost went in but fell out. "Come on, Ray, come on, Ray," everybody shouted. Ray took his time, sized up the hole, and placed himself so he could see right through the middle. He tossed. The bag hit the side but fell through. Everybody gathered around him to congratulate him. Jean-Paul said, "The best man won." Ray's other cousins agreed.

When the sack race, the beanbag toss, and other games were over, Ray, a winner in some, had a choice of a special CD, a gift certificate to his favorite fast-food place, or a book. Best of all, Ray felt more at ease with his cousins. He was now ready to hear Great-gran-papa tell the story of the family.

9

Toussaint!

IT WAS SO HOT Ray's clothes stuck to his back. He wondered if he would have time to shower and get ready for Great-gran-papa's storytelling. He rushed and had hardly finished dressing when there was a knock on the door. "Ray, it's your cousins Joel and Augustine. Come with us to hear Great-gran-papa."

Ray was so excited. "We had better hurry if we want to get a good place," Joel said.

"I don't remember much about this," Ray said.

"Everybody comes." Joel pulled Ray along.

Ray's video had let him in on Toussaint Breda; Christopher, the first emperor of Haiti; and Dessalines, the father of Haiti's independence. But he wanted to hear about the revolution from Great-gran-papa. He felt a tug of excitement and let Joel pull him along.

All of his young relatives were rushing to the same place. When he and Joel got there, the room was crowded. "Hey, Joel, Ramon, over here," Jean-Paul called. He had saved them a seat close up front. Good to have friends, Ray thought. He looked around the room. Marguerite was there with her friends. This was an event for the children, so not many adults were there. Those who were sat in chairs. The children sat on the floor in front of the chair placed for Great-gran-papa. And on the side, Gran-papa Philippe sat alone. Ray wished he were with him.

There was so much noise and excitement that Ray thought this must be something special. "What's all the fuss about?" he asked.

"You'll see," Jean-Paul said. "This, to me, is

the best part of the reunion."

"Even better'n the picnic?" Ray asked.

"Way better," Augustine said.

Great-gran-papa came into the room, and everybody stood and applauded. He responded. With his palms together on his chest, his fingers pointing toward his face, he bowed slightly to all sides of the room. Everyone sat and the room became utterly quiet. Great-gran-papa stood still, looking out at them. No one moved. The quiet to Ray was like a living presence, and he was startled when Great-gran-papa said with a strong voice, "And cric!"

"And crac!" they all shouted.

"Aha! You believe a good story is worth telling and you are ready to listen. And cric and crac," Great-gran-papa said.

"And mistic-crac!" they all cried.

"Listen, listen, and you will hear the heart-beat of your ancestors who, long ago, lived in the French West Indian colony of Saint Domingue. As captive people they were beaten, buried in the earth up to their heads, and left for the insects to torture. For sport, gunpowder was forced inside them and lighted to blow them to bits. But their masters insisted that they were happy."

"No. No!" the children cried.

"Yes. As slaves they were forbidden to come together, but they walked many miles to meet. And to cover up their plans of rebellion, they sang, danced, and held rituals. Boukman, a voodoo high priest, a tall, giant of a black man, was their leader. There were six thousand men.

"On the twenty-second of August, 1791, the plans were laid, everything in place. That night a storm raged. Thunder sounded like a thousand drums, and lightning licked the sky like snake tongues, and the silent island was alive with the secrets of the slaves.

"Was the storm a warning for them to call off the rebellion?" Great-gran-papa asked.

"Yes, yes, call it off!" some of the children cried.

"No! No!" others shouted.

Ray was listening so intently that he wanted them to get quiet so that the story could continue.

"The wind roared and the rain fell in sheets. Strange lights were seen in the thick forest of the mountain. On that very night, under lighted torches, Boukman and the leaders of the revolt made their final plan. When Boukman gave the last instructions, he prayed, 'Spirit who rules the waves and rides the winds and rain of storms, let us listen to the voice of liberty, which speaks to the hearts of us all.' The storm was their good omen."

Great-gran-papa paused, and Ray heard the deep breath that he, too, had taken just before the silence of the room returned.

"That very night the slaves who were considered the happiest slaves on earth led the way. They destroyed the masters and burned plantations to the ground. Everywhere plantation owners were surprised. How could these people who had been so happy do this?"

Again Great-gran-papa paused, and everyone waited.

"The revolt lasted. After a month of burning, Toussaint Breda joined them. Who was Toussaint Breda?"

The question was so unexpected that for a while nobody answered. Great-gran-papa waited. Ray's heart raced, and he was so excited that he could hardly speak. "One of the leaders of the revolution that created Haiti," he blurted out.

"Who said that?" Great-gran-papa asked. "Speak up, I can't hear you. Stand up."

Ray was so embarrassed. All eyes were on him. He couldn't move.

Joel and Jean-Paul were pushing him up. "Go on, go on."

Finally he stood and repeated what he had said.

"Oh, my namesake with the sugarcane," Great-gran-papa said. Everybody laughed. "And can you name the others?"

Ray took a deep breath, "Christopher, the first emperor of Haiti, and Dessalines, the father of Haiti's independence."

"Recognize him! Give him credit." Great-gran-papa led the applause.

When Ray sat down, he looked at Gran-papa Philippe. Gran-papa smiled and gave him two thumbs-up.

Great-gran-papa went on. "Toussaint Breda, a most unusual slave, a coachman, became a fearless leader who could do with two hours of sleep and for days eat only two bananas and drink water." Gran-papa looked out at them and asked, "What is the answer to the question, 'Who is he who will raise the standard of liberty?'?"

"Toussaint!" they all shouted.

"He won so many victories it was said of him, 'This man makes openings everywhere.' So he changed his name to Toussaint L'Ouverture, which means 'the opening.'

"With a leader who rode up front to face the enemy, many more slaves joined the revolt. Among them was our ancestor, Jean Baptiste Moret. The revolt turned into war. A terrible war not only against the French, but also against the Spaniards and the English, who wanted the rich island with thousands of slaves. The Africans wanted nothing less than freedom, and the war turned on that.

"Now you might wonder how we happen to

be here and not in Haiti. In 1793 Jean Baptiste Moret was in the army that swooped down upon the city of Le Cap. Two-thirds of the city was destroyed. More than ten thousand French refugees crowded onto boats in the harbor and fled to the French colony in America.

"Jean Baptiste Moret, an adventurous man, came with the flood of refugees, and landed in New Orleans. Claiming himself a free man, he moved into the French territory, Natchitoches. There he met and married the lovely daughter of Pierre Conant and Thérèse Unwa, Rose Marie. They had one son, Jean Baptiste, who married and had two children, Louis Toussaint and Mary Thérèse Moret. They and their descendants are the Morets who married Radcliffs and Baptistes. They drained the swamps, cleared the land, and built a prosperous Creole community that is now Morets, Radcliffs, and Baptistes. I salute you all!"

For a moment the room was quiet; then there was applause and an explosion of talk.

Everybody wanted to get close to Great-gran-papa. Ray joined his cousins and Marguerite, who all said *"Merci! Merci, Great-gran-papa*

Ramon." Gran-papa Philippe stood where he had been seated. Ray walked by and without looking at him said, "Early, Gran-papa." Ray looked back. Gran-papa smiled, and Ray knew they had a date.

10

Africa House

Early the next morning, Gran-papa Philippe was waiting for Ray. "Are you sure you want to do this? I don't like meeting you in secret, but I do want to show you something very special."

"I want to," Ray said almost in a whisper. He felt nervous and a little afraid. What if his papa woke up and looked for him? He moved fast to set the pace. They did not talk, and Ray felt that Gran-papa must have been a little worried, too. Finally Ray said, "How come he doesn't like you?"

"I think that is something that your papa must tell you. I came because my sister said that all of you would be here. I have longed to see you, and so I'm here. I want to show you who I am, not tell you."

"I want to know so much. How old are you?" Ray said, and Gran-papa laughed. "Where do you live? And why haven't you come to see us?"

"I'm as old as my tongue and a little older than my teeth," Gran-papa said.

"Aw, that's not fair. Tell me."

"I'm almost sixty-five, and I live not too far from here, in New Orleans." Then Gran-papa was quiet. Finally he said, "I called once and you answered the phone, remember? You know what happened." When Gran-papa did not say any more, Ray could see that he was uncomfortable.

They had entered the grounds of the plantation and passed the big house that Unwa's sons had built and where she had lived in her old age. "See those two houses over there?"

"They look like houses you see in pictures about Africa," Ray answered. The two-story house with one room on each floor had a big thatched roof shaped like a bowl turned upside down.

"Exactly. They look like no other houses in the area. I guess Unwa was remembering stories her papa and moman told her about houses in West Africa where they came from. The little one is called Ghana House; the bigger one is called Africa House. Unwa with her Creole sons built them with clay bricks they made with their own hands and with cypress trees that grew on their land.

"They lived in these small houses until they had cleared their land. With relatives and others that she bought out of slavery, Unwa and her sons carved the plantation out of the wilderness. They raised the best tobacco on the Red River and shipped it along with beef, bear grease, bear hides, and indigo down that river to New Orleans, and from there to France and to Spain."

From outside Ray could see there was a fireplace. "Can we go inside?"

"Of course."

Inside, Ghana House was moldy, ancient, and dark. Ray wondered how many people had lived in this little house with no windows. As if Gran-papa knew what Ray was thinking, he said, "Whole families lived in places smaller than this. They cooked their meals in iron pots hung over the fire right in the room where they all slept, ate, and did their living."

Then they went to Africa House. Ray followed Gran-papa Philippe inside. It had windows. With the heavy, low-hanging thatched roof that had protected it from the sun and rain, it didn't look as if it had been built more than a hundred and fifty years ago. This was the first house in which Unwa and her family lived.

"I've never seen a place like this before," Ray said.

"I hear there may be only one other one like it in the nation," Gran-papa said.

The place was wired for lighting. "It is a museum with very old things displayed in the rooms," Gran-papa said. "These rosary beads were made by Unwa for her daughter, Rose Marie."

"Rose Marie married Jean Baptiste Moret."

"You remember, ahn?"

"How could I forget, the way Great-gran-papa told it! I liked that."

"My papa is a great storyteller."

They walked up the stairs and suddenly Ray was surrounded by walls covered with paintings. Bold, bright colors mixed with the dark earth, dark clouds, dark water, and dark people like his African ancestors.

Ray went from wall to wall seeing life as it must have been when his ancestors owned and lived on this place. People were threshing pecan trees. Women were washing and hanging clothes on clotheslines. There were people hoeing tobacco and picking tobacco leaves. There were green leaves hanging and golden leaves carefully packed for storing. There were men on large rafts floating down the river with barrels marked BEAR GREASE and INDIGO, and there were bales of tobacco.

Ray walked around amazed, silent. Finally he asked, "Did children draw these pictures?"

"Oh, no!" Gran-papa answered.

"These are good. I like them; they remind me

of paintings some of my friends do."

"That's a compliment. This is what some people call primitive art. I call it heart-and-soul, not-messed-up-with-lessons, straight-from-the-imagination art."

On one whole wall there was a picture of rich, lush, green sugarcane. A huge wall of fire was approaching and burning here and there. Odious smoke billowed up, blanketing the earth with darkness.

"What is this?" Ray asked, alarmed.

"That is the Haitian revolt that Great-gran-papa was telling about."

There was another picture of a town's harbor with many boats anchored in the water. Red flames licked through a blanket of smoke and lit the sky. Ashes were falling on everything.

Gran-papa Philippe explained, "That is the town of Le Cap in Haiti the way it looked during the revolt. For three whole weeks, the people of the town could hardly tell night from day. Ashes from the straw of burning sugarcane fell, covering everything in the city, even ships in the harbor.

The harbor from which our ancestor sailed."

Thinking he had seen all the paintings, Ray was ready to leave Africa House. He looked up at the ceiling and cried, "Ooh!" Above, a black Christ on a white cross shocked him. At first all he saw was the Christ. Then on the left and right of the Christ he noticed two white thieves on black crosses.

In awe Ray whispered, "Gran-papa, look at that!" He had never seen anything like that and hadn't even dared think of such. *A black Christ!* Every Christ he had ever seen was white!

"That's *The Dark Crucifixion*," Gran-papa said.

"Do you like that painting, Gran-papa?"

"Do you?"

"I asked you first. But I don't know. I guess the painter wanted us to see how he sees things. And then let us decide if we see it like that, too."'

"Ramon, you are a smart boy. That's why I brought you here. I wanted you to see what I see that has meaning for me."

"Who made these paintings?"

"I did."

Suddenly Ray remembered, "A black Christ, for heaven sake." His tant and nonks were talking about his gran-papa!

Ray's scalp tingled as Gran-papa went on. "I started drawing when I was a boy younger than you. I did odd jobs around the Indigo Plantation when it was owned once by a writer. He brought writers and artists from all over the country to work here. I drew and painted on anything I could find, cardboard, wrapping paper, even wood boards. Some of the visitors liked my work and gave me a dollar and sometimes more for it. The owner paid me to do the work on the walls to represent the life of our ancestors on the plantation.

"When I was about sixteen, an artist came and when he left he gave me his supplies: brushes, paints, and canvass. With the paints I would slip in here and paint that ceiling. Nobody noticed. As you can imagine, then there wasn't much light in here. But the image was bright in my mind and I drew it.

"Finally the owner saw *The Dark Crucifixion*. He liked it, so he gave me some money for supplies and helped me sell some of the work that I did. I was on my way. . . ." Gran-papa was quiet, as if remembering those days. "Oh, my goodness," Grand-papa said, looking at his watch. "It's much later than I thought. We must get back."

Outside Ray saw that the sun was high in the sky. His family would certainly be worried about him. And if Papa found him with Gran-papa, there would be trouble.

"We better hurry," Ray said. "Maybe I should go back alone."

"No way. I will take you back to where I met you."

They had not gone far when Ray saw his family. He was so frightened. "Run, Gran-papa. Don't let him catch you with me," Ray said with tears in his voice.

"Don't, please don't be afraid. I won't let him hurt you. "

Ray's papa was seething with anger. "Old

man, I told you to stay away from my son." He was so close to Gran-papa Philippe that Ray thought his papa would hit him.

Ray, frightened, went to stand by Marguerite, feeling that he had caused all this trouble. Marguerite took his hand.

Gran-papa stood his ground.

Moman rushed up. "Louis, if you have no respect for your papa, then respect the children."

Gran-papa looked at Moman, touched her on the shoulder, and said, "No, let us have it out. What's on your mind, Louis?"

"You know what's on my mind. You've never been a papa to me. Never have. And now you want to come here pretending, hanging around him, filling him with I don't know what. It won't work. Come here, Ray."

Ray looked at Gran-papa and moved reluctantly toward his papa. Louis said, "Take a good look at him, for when you know how he treated me, you won't want to see him again. He left me when I was younger than you. I never heard from him. Not one word. My moman and his brother did everything for me. She wanted me to have the best and she worked to make it happen."

"Son—"

"Don't call me son." Again, Ray thought his papa would strike Gran-papa. Papa moved toward him, his fists clenched, with a scowl on his face. "Don't call me son! I'm the son of my mother, Suzette Rachal!"

Ray could see the pain in Gran-papa's face, but Gran-papa remained calm, listening to Papa. Finally, still calm, he said, "When you are ready to listen, I will tell you my side of the story." He walked away.

Ray stood, holding on tight to Marguerite. He felt sorry for his papa, but he was sorry for Gran-papa, too.

"Louis," Moman said, "I can understand your feelings. But you could at least give him a chance to talk to you."

"And you should see the paintings he did about the family," Ray said.

"So he impressed you, I see, but that doesn't impress me. It was the painting. That's all he wanted to do. All my uncles and cousins were well off. Moman and me? We had nothing. He was always so different. Like he shows up here in jeans and sandals. The artist. A no-money-making one. He deserted us. My uncles took care of me and Moman."

Ray was now torn. Maybe his papa was right not to see Gran-papa Philippe. But still he wanted to be with his gran-papa, too. What was it that his gran-papa wanted to tell his papa? He waited for someone to speak to get Papa to please give Gran-papa a chance.

"At least we could see the paintings, Papa," Marguerite said.

"Yes, we should see them," Moman said.

"If you're on his side, go. But I will not go."

Ray followed his family back to the hotel, angry with his papa and wondering why he could not listen to Gran-papa's side of the story. He felt that he had lost his gran-papa before he really got to know him.

Later Ray was alone with his papa. Thinking that maybe Papa was in a better mood and would understand how Ray felt, he said, "Papa, you should see the paintings. They are about our family. They're nice. You'll see."

"I will not go there, and I don't want to hear any more about that place and that man's paintings, you hear." Papa's anger returned.

Ray felt that he had made a mistake. Time was running out for him and Gran-papa Philippe.

11

Wishing for Another Encounter

THAT EVENING THE LAST event of the reunion was not at all exciting for Ray. Moman and Marguerite dressed up in their prettiest dresses and finest jewelry for the banquet and the dance. Ray in his suit and tie was uncomfortable. He looked all over for Gran-papa Philippe, but he was nowhere in sight. Maybe he had already left and gone back to New Orleans. I should have gotten his address, Ray thought. But it was too late now.

There was lots of food, but he was not

hungry. Jean-Paul and Joel wanted to know what was wrong. Ray said, "Nothing."

"It's something, man, what?" Joel asked.

"Nothing, I'm telling you, nothing."

They soon left him alone.

After the banquet the music was loud and lively. Marguerite was having a great time. All the cousins wanted to dance with her. Ray sat near the door, hoping that Gran-papa would come. Antoinette found him there. "I've been watching you. What's the matter? I think you've fallen under my Nonk Philippe's spell. I hope you're not sorry."

Ray looked at her and smiled. "I fell for him and I'm not sorry. I just hope he will come and see us."

"Maybe you'll see him again. Maybe not. But you've met him, and that's good. Me, I'm grateful for just a glimpse of my moman. So you hang in there."

"Antoinette, come dance with me," Nonk Dominique called. She was gone before Ray could ask what she meant. The evening ended with Ray wishing, but Gran-papa Philippe never came.

Ray lay in bed thinking about all that had happened. He was happy about winning and gaining applause from his cousins. Then he remembered the conversation with Antoinette about skin color, and what Marguerite had said about trying to protect him. He tried to focus just on winning, but his mind wandered to the paintings, especially *The Dark Crucifixion*. And then he remembered his papa's outburst of anger at Gran-papa Philippe. He tried to feel again the joy of winning, but his mind would not stay with that joy. He could hear his papa's voice saying over and over, "You're just like Gran-papa Philippe. . . . You even look like him."

What was so wrong that he spoke with such disgust when he said, "You even look like him!" What was wrong with looking like Gran-papa? "She didn't know what black meant. She probably had heard somebody say that word about somebody they didn't like, and maybe she didn't like Mark, but she liked you." Is black for someone you don't like? he said to himself.

He had been satisfied, and he was happy when his moman had explained why he looked the way he looked and said he was creating a beautiful person. But now! Why was he feeling so ashamed? Guilty! Why did Marguerite need to protect him? From what?

Then suddenly the question that he had not wanted to ask came forcefully into his mind: Does Papa love me? How could he? I am like Gran-papa, and Papa hates him. He hates me, too! Hot tears rolled down his cheeks as he wondered what he could do.

❖   ❖   ❖

Sunday morning, the last day of the reunion, Ray got out of bed and dressed quietly. Late that afternoon they would be flying home. Although his family was not going to early Mass, Ray decided to go, hoping that Gran-papa Philippe would be there.

Outside, the sun was already burning hot, even though it was early. The quiet of Sunday filled the space that was usually occupied by the bustle of people and the hum of city traffic. He walked with the others, mostly elders with their heads carefully covered, to the small church. Ray waited outside, hoping that Gran-papa would arrive. He waited. Just before the service began, he went inside without him.

After the service a few of the families toured the grounds and went into Africa House to see the paintings. Ray wondered what they would say about his gran-papa's work. But disappointed that Gran-papa was not there, he walked back toward the hotel.

Nonk Antoine and his wife walked just ahead of Ray on the path back. Ray heard Antoine say, "I don't know why some of this family would go into Africa House that's been made unholy by Philippe."

"Some of them don't even know what unholy is," his wife said.

"Yeah, you're right. I'm just glad we're not part of that group," Antoine said.

Ray listened and began to understand a little bit better now why some of the relatives did not like his gran-papa. However, he knew that no matter what his papa and the others thought, he loved Gran-papa and would try to let him know that he wanted him in his life. Maybe he has already gone back to New Orleans, Ray thought as he walked back to the hotel to pack for his journey home.

12

À Bientôt, Gran-papa!

THE ROOM WAS EMPTY when Ray returned. Marguerite had packed her bag and was probably with Mary Louise and Antoinette. He lay on the bed, wondering if Gran-papa would leave without saying good-bye. He thought of Antoinette and wished he could have gotten to know her better. The reunion was too short, he thought.

He got up and packed his clothes halfheartedly. He did not want to leave without having said good-bye to Gran-papa. Suddenly he had an idea. If Gran-papa were still in Natchitoches, he would certainly be at Africa House with the paintings.

Ray hurried, throwing things into the suitcase without care, and rushed to the river. All was quiet. He followed the now-familiar path past the cotton field through the pecan orchard, on to Indigo Plantation. Now no one was at Africa House, and there seemed to be nothing alive at the place. Of course, it was still early. Later there would probably be tourists on the grounds.

He opened the door and cried out louder than he had thought, "Gran-papa, you in there?" Only the echo of his voice answered. He waited just outside the opened door. Finally, disappointed, he quietly closed the door.

He felt that he had wasted his time. If Gran-papa really wanted to see him, he thought, he would have come to the hotel. He knew Ray was there. If Gran-papa didn't care, then who would? His chest felt heavy, and tears that would not flow filled his throat.

He looked around at the houses and buildings that his ancestor Unwa had built with her French Creole children. Children who had looked like Marguerite, his papa, Antoinette, and Antoinette's moman, Ramona. Did any of them resemble Unwa, the way Gran-papa Philippe is like her and the way I look like him?

He hurried back to the hotel, still feeling sad. Just as he passed the cotton field, near the river, he saw his papa. This time he was not afraid. Anger took control and he no longer felt the tears. Where was he going? Ray wondered. Had he come because he thought Ray would be with Gran-papa Philippe? He need not fear that, Ray thought. Gran-papa was not going to risk his son's wrath again.

"I thought I'd find you here," Papa said without anger in his voice.

Ray was surprised and said hopefully, "So you want to go to the place where our ancestors lived?"

"I lived in this town when I was a boy, and the place holds few pleasant memories for me."

"Did you see the paintings?"

"No. My moman suffered because of those

paintings. That's how Mr. Philippe, as she called him, got his start. From then on he spent all of his time painting when he should have, like his brother, been working, earning good money to take care of us. She didn't like those paintings, and so I never saw them."

Ray looked at his papa pleadingly and said, "You could now."

"You don't listen," his papa shouted angrily. "You know this is something I don't talk about. I have said more to you than *anybody* about this matter. Can't you understand?"

"I understand." Ray could feel the heaviness in his chest return and his throat tightening. He stood still, head down. The anger he had felt before returned. "I understand you don't love me and it's because I'm black like Gran-papa Philippe."

The look on his papa's face frightened Ray. It was as though he had been struck. "Oh, no, how can you say that? I know I'm not the hugging kind, Ray, but I have been there for you, and I'll always be there, because I love you. This has nothing to do with color. This has nothing to do with you. It's the way *he* is!"

"But you don't like him."

"Is this what he has put into your head?"

"No. You. You always say I'm just like him. I even look like him and you hate him. So I think you hate me, too."

Just then Ray saw Gran-papa Philippe walking toward them, going toward the plantation. Ray ran to meet him. He threw his arms around his waist and said, "Oh, Gran-papa, I thought you had gone away."

"No, no, I wouldn't leave you without saying good-bye."

His papa came over to them and said, "I don't know what you have said to Ray about me—"

Gran-papa interrupted him. "Only that *you* must tell him why you don't want me to see him."

"I have told him and he understands. Let's go, Ray."

"I see you are not ready to listen to my side of the story." He opened the pouch and took out a packet. "For years I have saved this, hoping that I would see you and let you know what happened. I admit I was not the person that your moman could be happy with. We did not see eye to eye. She liked lots of expensive things that meant little to me. So she left. I have regretted that I didn't understand then and try harder to give her more. Because I didn't try, I lost you. I hope when you know that I tried to be in touch with you, you will understand." He offered Louis the packet. Louis would not take it. Granpapa put it on the ground and walked away.

Ray remembered what Moman and Marguerite had said about Gran-moman. How sharp she was. Liked expensive things. Hats and gloves. Ray knelt and looked inside the pouch.

There were photographs of his papa when he was a boy, and paintings of him, some yellowed with age, and many unopened returned letters. Ray began to open them. His papa became curious and looked at some, too. As Ray read, he realized that many had been mailed on his papa's birthday every year since Papa and

Gran-moman had left Gran-papa Philippe. There were cash or money orders in the older ones and checks in the later ones.

"Look, Papa," Ray said, "this one was sent on your eighteenth birthday. It says:

> *Today in the eyes of the law, you're a man. But I see you as you were the last time I saw you, a boy, only a promise of a man. Forgive me. I regret that I have missed seeing that promise realized. Please know that I love you. I hope that all is well with you and that we will be in touch soon.*
>
> *Papa*

Ray handed the letter to his papa. Louis read it and said, "I don't believe this." Ray and his papa stood in the silence. Then Papa said, "Moman had her reasons for returning them." The soft lapping of the river was the only sound. Finally Ray said, "Papa, you really should see the paintings."

"Perhaps I should. But not without your moman and Marguerite."

❈   ❈   ❈

When Ray and his family arrived at Africa House, the lights were on. Ray opened the door and shouted, "Anybody here?"

Gran-papa answered, "Only an old man alone. Do come in."

Ray saw the surprise on Gran-papa's face when they all entered.

"Gran-papa, my papa has come. This is my moman, Camolia, and my sister, Marguerite."

Ray saw the tears of joy in Gran-papa's eyes as he embraced Marguerite, then Moman. He stood before his son, seemingly not knowing what to do or say. Papa held out his arms for the longest embrace with his father.

There were tears aplenty, and many oohs and ahs when they joined Marguerite upstairs to look at the paintings and found her staring at *The Dark Crucifixion*. "Gran-papa, how did you come to do this picture? I don't believe Christ is black," she said.

"In my painting he is. And when you know

where he lived, it is not hard to imagine his being black."

There was silence. Ray could feel that his moman and papa were embarrassed and did not want to talk about that painting. He pointed at the painting of burning sugarcane fields and said, "Look, Papa." His father moved to look more closely at the painting. After another long moment, he said, "Yes. Great-gran-papa's vision of the Haitian revolution."

The tension relieved, Papa and Moman moved to talk to Gran-papa Philippe. Ray was overwhelmed with joy, knowing that he had helped bring his family together. When it was time for them to leave, Gran-papa put his arm around Ray's shoulder. He looked up at his son and said, "Louis, I am proud to see that you have a strong family."

Ray embraced his gran-papa and said, "Good-bye."

"Every shut-eye ain't sleep, every good-bye ain't gone," Papa said. "Don't say good-bye. Say 'À bientôt'! I promise you'll see your gran-papa again."

Ray embraced his papa and said, "This is the best reunion ever. In this room with my family and all of our ancestors, I feel that I have come home."

Author's Note

❧

The story here is fiction. It is set where the original Creoles of Louisiana lived and carved a place on the Cane River. The houses described in the story exist in Natchitoches, Louisiana, on the grounds of Melrose Plantation. There are paintings on the walls and the ceiling depicting life during the early days of African Americans, painted by the well-known artist Clementine Hunter. In 1974 the estate grounds of the Melrose Plantation were declared a national historic landmark in recognition of the unusual architecture of several of the buildings there. Any similarities to names and persons is coincidental.

Glossary of Creole Words

à bientôt	see you soon
byen, bon	good
et	and
frèr	brother
gran-moman	grandmother
gran-papa	grandfather
kouzen (m.) *kouzin* (f.)	cousin
maten	morning
mo cheri (m.) *ma cherie* (f.)	my dear
moman	mother
nonk	uncle
papa	father
parkwa	welcome
parle kréyol	speak Creole
sa	he
sa tchòb byen	how goes it
tant	aunt
te (m.) *ta* (f.)	your
tro	too
vou, to	you

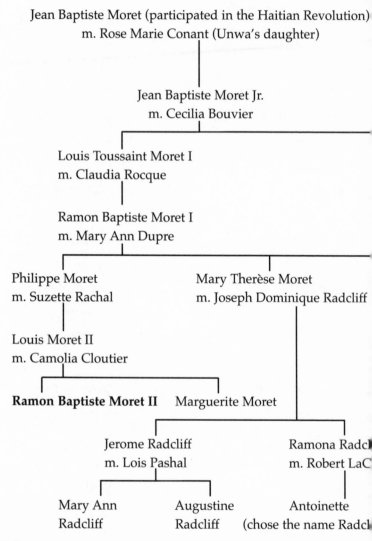

Jean Baptiste Moret (participated in the Haitian Revolution)
m. Rose Marie Conant (Unwa's daughter)

Jean Baptiste Moret Jr.
m. Cecilia Bouvier

Louis Toussaint Moret I
m. Claudia Rocque

Ramon Baptiste Moret I
m. Mary Ann Dupre

Philippe Moret
m. Suzette Rachal

Mary Therèse Moret
m. Joseph Dominique Radcliff

Louis Moret II
m. Camolia Cloutier

Ramon Baptiste Moret II   Marguerite Moret

Jerome Radcliff
m. Lois Pashal

Ramona Radc
m. Robert LaC

Mary Ann
Radcliff

Augustine
Radcliff

Antoinette
(chose the name Radc

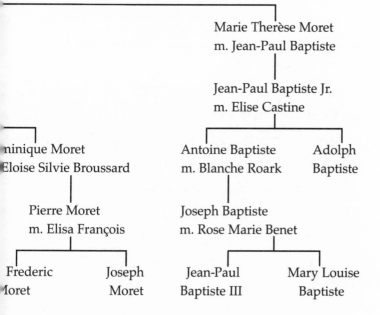

Marie Thérèse Moret
m. Jean-Paul Baptiste

Jean-Paul Baptiste Jr.
m. Elise Castine

ninique Moret
Eloise Silvie Broussard

Antoine Baptiste
m. Blanche Roark

Adolph
Baptiste

Pierre Moret
m. Elisa François

Joseph Baptiste
m. Rose Marie Benet

Frederic
Moret

Joseph
Moret

Jean-Paul
Baptiste III

Mary Louise
Baptiste

About the Author

Mildred Pitts Walter is a ground-breaking author who began writing children's books while working in California during the early 1960s. A teacher who reviewed books for the *Los Angeles Times*, she had been able to find only a few books by and for African Americans. When Mildred questioned a publisher about the lack of books for African-American children, she was asked to write one.

Beginning with her first book, LILLIE OF WATTS, in 1969, Mildred Pitts Walter has crafted highly regarded novels and picture books that portray the strength and complexity of family relationships. Mildred has a particular gift for writing about young African-American boys; perhaps her keen feeling comes from being the mother of two boys as well as a loving grandmother. JUSTIN AND THE BEST BISCUITS IN THE WORLD, one of her most popular books, won the Coretta Scott King Award for Fiction. *Publishers Weekly* called it "a warm, funny story of a boy's struggle to become a 'man' in a family of females. . . . Refreshing, likable characters, an exciting rodeo, and a history of the black cowboys combine to create a very special story." MY MAMA NEEDS ME, a picture book inspired by one of her grandsons, with artwork by Pat Cummings, won the Coretta Scott King Award for Illustration. In addition, she has received Coretta Scott King Honor Awards for her novels BECAUSE WE ARE and TROUBLE'S CHILD, and the Christopher Award for MISSISSIPPI CHALLENGE, the gripping nonfiction account of the civil rights movement in Mississippi.

Mildred Pitts Walter lives in Denver, Colorado.